For Angelo Tripodi, gladiator and father-in-law.

I would like to dedicate the entire Gladiator Boy *series
to Terry Pratchett. There is no writer, living or dead,
for whom I have greater respect. Thank you
for everything.*

GLADIATOR BOY

A HERO'S QUEST

GLADIATOR BOY

A HERO'S QUEST

DAVID GRIMSTONE

Hodder
Children's
Books

A division of Hachette Children's Books

UNIVERSITY OF CHICHESTER

CONTENTS

ANCIENT ITALY

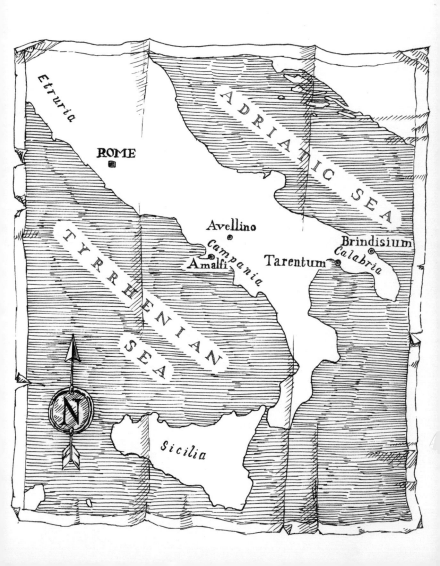

CHAPTER
I

TAKEN

When Decimus Rex awoke, he was plunged into a world of darkness and deafening noise. As his battered senses adjusted to their new surroundings, the darkness became a covering made from some sort of animal hide and the noise became the low and thunderous rumbling of a wagon.

Decimus wasn't the sort of boy who cried in a difficult situation. He felt pain and despair like anyone else, but he was able to hold his fear inside. His father had taught him at a young age that crying never solved anything, and he had taken the lesson to heart. What mattered were facts, and the fact was he had been taken from his parents' house by men who had knocked him unconscious and

thrown him in the back of this wagon.
Moreover, his father must have witnessed the
entire event: he'd been standing only a few feet
away when it happened.

Decimus felt a sudden panic rise within
him, and had to bunch his hands into fists to
stop them shaking. He tried to grit his teeth
and summon some energy, but it seemed to

require a colossal effort even to turn his head. When he tried to take a deep breath, his chest reacted with a sharp stabbing pain. He needed to think, and to clear his head . . . but he was too afraid, and his mind was too clouded with questions. If these people had bundled him into a wagon . . . what had they done to his father? The thought was quickly followed by others. How long had he been asleep? Minutes? Hours? It was hard to tell – he could be halfway to Rome by now.

Before he could raise himself on to his elbows, a noise in the corner of the cart caused Decimus to start: he quickly scrambled backwards, his eyes locked on the shifting shadows.

'Is someone there?'

'Yeah,' said a sad voice, which sounded as though it had fought tears ... and lost. 'They took me, too. You've been out for ages – I thought they might have killed you or something. I'd just woken up when they brought you in.'

'I'm not injured: at least, I don't think so. My chest hurts, though. What about you; are you hurt?'

'No, but I'm scared.'

'Me too. My name's Decimus, by the way: Decimus Rex.'

'I'm Gladius. I come from Brindisium: it's ... it's my birthday tomorrow.'

Decimus could hear from the change in his new companion's voice that the boy's tears

were about to resurface, so he quickly tried
to divert his attention.

'You were taken from Brindisium? That's
in Calabria, isn't it?'

'Yeah ... it's been a long journey.'

'Are you tied up?'

'Yeah.'

'By your feet, I'm guessing. I think we
might both be chained to this iron ring near

me. If I can just—'

The wagon juddered over a rocky section of road, throwing the two boys around like a couple of pebbles inside a sack. Decimus winced as his head slammed into the side of the wagon, while Gladius badly bruised his elbow on a broken wheel that had been tossed inside by their captors shortly after he'd been taken.

'Don't bother,' said Gladius, nursing his arm. 'I tried to break out when they stopped at Tarentum to get you – there's no chance. Those chains are solid, and they're fastened to a block of wood that's thicker than my leg.'

Decimus doubted that; from what he could make out, the young boy lying in the shadows opposite him was huge.

'Who ARE they?' said Gladius, shifting slightly as the wagon hit yet another rut in the road. 'Why did they take us?'

Decimus hunkered down beside the rough wood and tried to wedge himself into the corner of the wagon so he could see a bit more of the inside.

'Are you rich?' he said. 'Your parents, I mean?'

'No,' said Gladius. 'My father works for a sea trader who ports at Brindisium; he doesn't earn much from it. What about you?'

'My dad carries messages between the merchant houses in Tarentum,' said Decimus, evenly. 'If neither of us are rich and we're both from different towns, my guess is we've been snatched by slave-takers.'

A heavy silence settled over the cart as it turned slightly and started off along a new road.

'S-slave-takers?' Gladius said, eventually. 'B-but what does that mean?'

'It means we're slaves,' said Decimus, without the slightest trace of fear in his voice. 'And don't bother crying, either – crying is a waste of energy. My dad taught me all about slave-takers: they have no mercy.'

'B-but why us? What did we do wrong?'

Decimus took a deep breath and exhaled, his neck beginning to ache.

'We didn't do anything wrong, Gladius: we were just unlucky. As for why they took us, well . . . it really depends who they are. The Brindisium gangs always take slaves to sell food for them in Rome, the Tarentiums get theirs to dig ditches. Personally, I hope it's one of them – that way, we've got a good chance of escape. The only other slave-takers are the ones from Campania . . . and believe me, we better HOPE we haven't been taken by them.'

Even though they were several feet apart, Decimus could hear Gladius gulp.

'W-why? What do they use slaves for?'

'They train them to fight,' said the young captive, his eyes locked on the large shadow opposite him, '. . . in The Arena.'

As the hours passed and the wagon rolled on, Decimus became more and more certain that they were heading for Campania. He and Gladius talked little on the remaining journey, and both boys drifted off to sleep several times before the wagon finally rumbled to a halt.

Suddenly, the great hide covering was ripped open and a heavily muscled arm reached into the wagon and took hold of the wooden block that supported their chains. The veined hand fiddled with a noisy lock before, to their horror, Decimus and Gladius were dragged out of the wagon feet first. Both boys were hauled across the dusty ground, kicking and screaming, until the powerful arm released them.

Instinctively, Decimus rolled over and tried to stand, but tripped on the chain and collapsed in a heap. Gladius didn't even get that far. The boy, who Decimus could now see in the flickering torchlight was very overweight, couldn't seem to haul himself off the dirt. Instead, he just lay there, groaning and rubbing his head.

Amid the captors, a giant of a man with a blazing torch and an enormous broadsword barked orders and employed the blade to point in various directions. As the many hooded figures began to step back into the shadows, Decimus quickly saw that he and Gladius were only two of an incredible number of children gathered in the vast stretch of barren land that surrounded them.

'Where—'

Gladius made to say something, but Decimus noted the expression on the big man's face and quickly jabbed his new friend in the ribs to keep him quiet. Then he glanced around them. At first, he thought there might be hundreds of children in the circle that had been formed by the captors. Then, as his eyes adjusted to the fiery darkness, he began to count heads.

He'd reached fifty, all boys of a similar age to themselves, when a deep, booming voice rang out over the sobs and screams of the captives.

'My name,' said the bearded giant, 'is Tiberius. However, if you should address me by my name, you will be soundly beaten. You will call me Master.'

A hushed silence had settled over the gathered boys, and there wasn't a single whisper to be heard. Decimus felt the hairs on his neck begin to rise.

'You have been brought here because your families have amassed a debt to Slavious Doom, Overlord of Campania. Some of you – a lucky few – will earn the right to settle those debts in service to the overlord, by entertaining his guests in the arena. The rest of you, those found wanting, will be imprisoned until your families are able to fund your release.'

The giant held aloft the torch and a disgusting grin spread across his face. 'Do not hold out much hope of release, my boys: a hundred Denarii gets added to the debt for every day you rot in your cells. You now belong to Slavious Doom: ALL of you. Hahahahaha!'

Decimus absorbed the information without question: he knew his family had always been poor and it wasn't impossible that his father had amassed such a debt, he knew.

Beside him, Gladius was taking in the scene with a mixture of horror and disgust.

One thing was certain: the boy was in no state to work or fight for his family's debt – poor Gladius would have to trust to luck to save his skin. Looking around once again, Decimus could see many different boys: some lean and muscular, but many ragged-looking and several who seemed, like Gladius, fat of stomach and very sluggish. None of them looked as though they could muster much of a fight, and very few looked capable of digging even the smallest ditch.

Decimus returned his attention to the giant, who had passed his torch to one of the captors and was cupping both hands around his mouth.

'You will rest for an hour,' he cried. 'After that, your beams will be chained together and you will march west to a place that many of you, in time, will learn to call home. Prepare yourselves: at Arena Primus you will all, for good or for ill, face your destinies. Do not ask questions of us: I have told you what is necessary. Enjoy this short break – you will need it! Hahahaha!'

The booming laugh erupted once again, and the giant moved over to whisper to his brutal companions.

'We're dead,' Gladius whispered, his face contorted in fear. 'We're all dead.'

Decimus shook his head. 'We'll be OK,' he said, cracking his jaw. 'You and me, both: as long as we stick together.

CHAPTER II

ARENA OF DEATH

The march to Arena Primus was long and gruelling, and more than once Decimus suspected his friend would collapse before they reached their goal. As it was, the snaking line of young slaves actually helped to support each other, and the line of wooden beams became not just dead weight but a force driving them on.

The arena itself was nothing like Decimus had imagined. His father had told him of the bustling amphitheatre in Rome, of the

chariot racing and the battles between men and wild beasts, of halls decorated with sculptures and murals, of colourful servants offering lark's tongues and peacock brains to the hungry, roaring crowd.

The only thing Arena Primus seemed to have in common with the amphitheatre was size: it was vast in a way Decimus simply couldn't comprehend, and seemed to stretch off in every direction. His heart thumped in his chest at the sight, but a voice inside his

head told him that the arena only appeared so immense because it was empty: rows of vacant stalls conspired to make the place even more alien than it seemed. The pit itself was a colossal circle filled with sand and punctuated, at its northern and eastern

points, by large iron portcullises.
Decimus noted that one of these
obviously led to the
outside world;

the other, he assumed, barred the way into the depths of the arena's hidden areas.

Somewhat surprisingly, Gladius hadn't stopped talking since they'd arrived. Decimus thought this might be because the boy was so incredibly relieved that the walking was over. Either way, he was suddenly very animated.

'Do you think we'll get to watch the events?' he said, peering around them as the portcullis through which they had emerged slammed to the ground. 'I've always wanted to see a contest, myself, but we could never afford to go. Do you think we—'

'I think you better shut up,' Decimus snapped, nodding past his friend at a muscled thug who was progressing along the line of slaves and unlocking their various chains.

'They're letting us go?' Gladius continued, confused. 'But aren't they worried that we might escape?'

'Through those?' Decimus exclaimed, pointing toward the north and east portcullises. 'No, I don't think they're worried at all. What's more, great Gladius, I don't think you fully understand what's going on here. We're going to see the games, all right . . . because we're going to be in them . . . or else, we're going to rot in some stinking cell, probably underground in the damp, dark places they put children to forget about them.'

Gladius smiled weakly, as if he thought his stern companion might be joking.

When he realized Decimus was deadly serious, the smile soon slid off his face.

'I don't think I'll be much good at games,' he said. 'I never catch anything my dad throws at me.'

Decimus reached out an arm and patted Gladius gently on the shoulder.

'These probably aren't going to be the sort of games where they throw a ball at you,' he muttered. 'And if they do, you can bet it will be covered in spikes.'

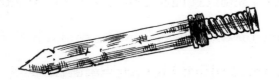

In the hours that followed, Decimus and Gladius learned a lot about their new surroundings. The arena basically comprised five sections, including the animal pits, the arena floor, the trial-master's quarters, the amphitheatre and the prison cells in which they would be staying until their families' debts were earned back.

Decimus also learned, by lingering at the back of the slave-line, that there were sixty-four boys in total . . . and the trial-master was expecting to lose at least ten of those the following day.

'Lose?' Gladius gasped when Decimus relayed the overheard conversation. 'What do they mean, exactly?'

Decimus rolled his eyes, but made an effort to keep his voice level: he knew Gladius was still deeply scared. 'It means the first trial will take place tomorrow, and they expect ten or more of us to fail it. If we do, we stay in jail.'

And what a jail it was.

Decimus and Gladius stepped reluctantly into their new home and stared about them. Two half-shattered wooden frames supported several bags of cloth stuffed with hay. Apart from these sparse features and a rough wooden bucket that didn't need any further explanation, the cell was empty. It was one of a row of three cells in this part of the prison, each separated by a row of thick iron bars.

'At least we can see everything,' said Gladius, smiling nervously as he noted the lack of solid walls. 'You know, the jailer, some of the other slaves, when they bring us

food and stuff . . .'

'You think that's a good thing?' Decimus
said, when the large, pot-bellied jailer had

slammed the iron door behind them. 'It also means they can see EVERYTHING we do, so we have absolutely no chance of escape.'

Moreover, the other boys in their section didn't look too friendly. The cell immediately next to theirs contained a muscular youth of oriental origin and a pale, freckled youth who simply had to be a Gaul. In the cell next to that, a tall dark boy stared around him with wild eyes, seemingly taking in everything except his own cellmate, a greasy-looking character he'd heard some of the jailers refer to as 'the Etrurian'. He noted that none of them made any effort to speak, even to their own companions.

It was night before the food arrived, and Decimus wasn't surprised to see a bowl of something that looked like soup that had been left for days to congeal. Gladius nearly wept when the bowl was thrown down in front of him, especially as their cell was at the end of the corridor and they had been served last.

'Sorry to see your friend doesn't like the food,' said a voice, as the jailer departed.

Decimus looked up sharply, quickly trying to determine who had spoken. However, finding the culprit wasn't a difficult task: the Gaul was staring at them with a sarcastic smirk on his face.

'What's it to you?' Decimus barked, as Gladius lowered himself on to the hay-sacks and tried to make himself disappear.

'Nothing,' said the Gaul. 'I just don't think he's going to last very long, that's all.'

Decimus shrugged. 'And you think you will?'

'Maybe.'

'There's no point starting trouble,' said the Etrurian, his voice carrying from the far end of the cell corridor. 'There will be enough of that in the arena tomorrow.'

'I wasn't starting trouble,' said Decimus, defensively. 'He made a comment about my friend, and I was just replying to it.'

'I don't mind,' said Gladius quickly, his

eyes imploring Decimus not to make things worse. 'REALLY. I get teased for my size all the time.'

'Look,' the Etrurian continued. 'We're all in the same section, so the least we can do is put up with each other. If we can't manage that, it will be hell in here ... and we'll get hell in the arena.'

Decimus nodded.

'Agreed,' he said, clearly impressed by the Etrurian slave. 'I am Decimus Rex. This is

my friend, Gladius. As you can see, we're in the same situation as you.'

Gladius peered around and nodded a careful greeting at the four inmates who were staring in their direction.

'I am Ruma,' said the Etrurian. He pointed at his cellmate. 'This is Olu.'

The Gaul kicked a hay-sack aside and took a seat on the edge of the wooden bed-frame. 'I'm Argon, this is Teo, but it's the only thing he's told me so far: he's not

much of a talker.'

Decimus flashed a brief smile at the oriental, and then sat down on the floor and began to spoon generous portions of the foul-smelling soup into his mouth.

'These cells aren't so bad,' Argon said loudly, packing his hay-sacks inside the wooden frame until he'd fashioned a workable mattress. 'Do you think—'

'No, they aren't,' Ruma interrupted, as if reading the Gaul's mind.

Argon looked up, startled. 'You didn't even wait—'

'I didn't need to. You were going to say you wondered whether these cells are the ones we end up in if we fail the trials – and the answer is no. These are holding cells:

the permanent ones will be underground, probably dark, dank and a lot worse than this.'

Gladius paused with the soup spoon halfway to his mouth.

'How do you know all this?' he asked.

Ruma shrugged. 'I listen.'

'You listen well,' said Decimus, tipping the last of the soup into his mouth. 'For an Etrurian, at least.' He finished with a smile that he hoped wasn't unfriendly. Ruma didn't seem to take offence. Instead, he settled down to sleep.

'I don't suppose you managed to listen to any details of tomorrow's trial, did you?'

Ruma inclined his head slightly, and finally returned the smile.

'I wish,' he said.

CHAPTER III

THE TRIALS BEGIN

Decimus was surprised when he woke up naturally. He had expected to be shaken awake at some ungodly hour and thrown out in the early darkness to face an onslaught of rampaging lions or worse. Instead, his eyes flickered open and he yawned loudly, taking several moments to peer around blearily and force himself off the hay-sacks he was lying on.

On the other side of the cell, he saw that Gladius was still spread out on his own makeshift bed, snoring loudly. In the neighbouring cell, Argon and Teo were also sound asleep.

Forcing himself on to his feet, Decimus was surprised to see that the third cell was a hive of activity. Olu was practising some sort of headstand against the back wall while Ruma, the gangly Etrurian, was proceeding through a seemingly endless assortment of exercises. Decimus swore under his breath, cursing his own lack of activity. He didn't doubt that the two slaves' lively morning workout would prepare them well for the day ahead.

During the next half-hour, the remaining three slaves all began to stir, but Decimus took no notice. He had moved over to the front of the cell and was trying to see further along the corridor. He could just make out a table and the distant shape of the jailer who seemed to be in charge of their section. At length, he realized that the shape was getting bigger, and that the man was progressing toward him, stopping at every cell to dish out what was presumably yet another bowl of the wretched broth. Ruma and Olu stopped exercising to collect theirs, and Argon and Teo both struggled over to the bars. As the jailer approached, Decimus noticed that a ragged little dog ran beside him, trying to lick up any droplets of soup that missed the bowl and getting kicked several times for its trouble. The dog's yelping was evidently helping to wake Gladius, who rolled over and flopped on to the floor.

'Argh! Where am I? What's that noise?'

Decimus ignored his friend, and stepped back from the cell door as

the jailer moved to stand in front of it.

He was a large man with a few scrubby patches of beard and several missing teeth.

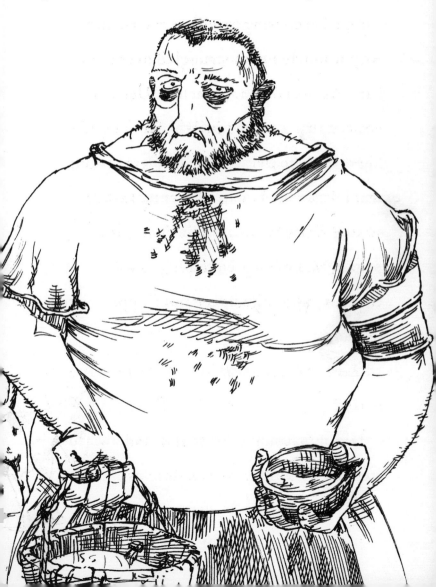

Up close, the dog appeared to be full of mange and undoubtedly hosted an entire community of fleas.

''ere,' he spat, shoving a bowl through the bars with such force that half the contents slopped out over the sides. Sensing the wasted soup, the little dog charged the bars, almost forcing its scruffy head between them in a desperate attempt to lick up the drops. Another sharp kick sent it skidding along the corridor, moaning and whining as it went.

Decimus accepted the bowl that was offered to him and returned to his bed.

The jailer turned and shuffled off up the corridor, pausing briefly to glance over his shoulder.

'Skrag – get 'ere now!'

The little dog finished licking its back leg and hurried to catch up with its master.

An hour passed without event, and Decimus guessed it was approaching mid-morning. He was just about to say as much to Gladius when the toothless jailer reappeared at the head of the corridor.

'Listen up, rags! I'm not goin' through this any more 'an I 'ave to! My name is Jailer Truli, or jus' Truli if yer feelin' brave! Every mornin', 'bout this time, I'll come down an' let you all out o' yer cells. When I open the door, you will all walk to the end o' the corridor an' turn righ' and walk t'ward the light – you turn left an' you'll soon regret it! When yer all assembled out on the arena floor, the trial-masters take over and give ya yer orders. Now, let's get you all movin'!'

Truli unlocked the first door and Decimus could see two slaves emerge into the corridor. His stomach was beginning to bunch up: the trials were about to start.

As Decimus and Gladius emerged on to the hot sand of the arena floor, they both realized two things very quickly. First, that

sixty-four
slaves
really didn't
look many in
the gaping
space they now
occupied and
secondly that the
trials were going to be
grim. The latter thought
occurred when a group of
men emerged carrying braziers full of
burning coals, which they proceeded to pour
on to the sand, moving around the perimeter
of the arena floor while the jailers quickly
ushered the slaves into the centre.

A short distance away, three men jumped

down from the lowest row of stalls and began to march across the sand. They were all very different in appearance: one was short and immensely fat, one was tall and practically stick thin, and the other was considerably older than his companions and covered in a network of ugly scars.

'I am Master Mori!' screamed the fat man, cupping his hands to his mouth. The sheer strength of his voice seemed to drive the slaves back, and several of the boys walked into each other.

Mori held up a hand and gestured toward the beanpole. 'This is Master Hrin and, on my other side,

Master Falni. We will be setting your trials until you leave Arena Primus. As you can see from the stalls, your trials will be unobserved. You are not worthy of an audience . . . yet. Form a line here NOW!'

Master Mori waddled a little way from his companions and held out his right hand. The slaves quickly formed a line, while Hrin and Falni wandered up and down, roughly spinning the boys around so that they were all facing the same way.

'This first test is one of endurance!' Mori continued. 'You will run around the edge of the arena. BAREFOOT.'

Decimus immediately reached down to unclasp his sandals, trying to ignore the worried whimpers Gladius was making as he performed the same task.

'You currently number sixty-four boys,' Mori yelled again. 'You will run until fifty remain. Those that fall will be eliminated from the trials.'

A series of gasps and mutterings erupted from the line: all were ignored by the trial-masters. Hrin and Falni retreated to the lower stalls, while Mori moved into the middle of the arena.

'Psst!' Decimus reached out and took hold

of Gladius's arm, dragging him close. 'Listen to me, and make sure you listen well. Work your way to the back, let one person overtake you at a time, and slow yourself right down. Do NOT run too fast. If they hit you, or whip you, or do anything to move you on, pretend to pick up the pace . . . but do NOT run fast, no matter WHAT happens. Understand?'

'But—'

'You'll run out of energy too soon – the heat and the effort will bring you down faster than a hail of spears. Trust me – save your strength.'

Gladius gawped at the sudden and terrible ferocity in his new friend's eyes: all he could do was to nod in agreement.

Mori screamed a command, and the line of slaves began to move, slowly at first . . . and then with increasing speed.

Decimus was among the last thirty boys. As he jogged along, trying to maintain a steady rhythm by repeating a rhyme over and over in his head, he tried to spot familiar faces in the curving line of boys. He concentrated hard, especially when his foot

landed on the first coal and he almost fell.
The burning of his flesh felt like an
explosion of pure agony . . . but he still
jogged on.

Concentrate, he told himself. Block out
the pain.

Then he saw Teo, close to the front,
hopping back and forth in a failed attempt to
avoid the coals while setting the pace for

those slaves racing up behind him. His gaze was still fixed on Teo when the first slave fell.

A scream pierced the air, and a boy two places back from the front of the line collapsed into the dirt, his body twitching and writhing as the coals began to burn him. As Decimus looked on, his eyes widening as he ran, two muscular servants snatched the slave up and carried him away.

Decimus almost cried out himself when his feet found yet another crop of burning coals, but he managed to right himself quickly enough to avoid stumbling. Other boys weren't so lucky, and a veritable cacophony of tortured screams erupted as the coals claimed several new victims.

Decimus didn't dare look back over his shoulder, but he felt certain that Gladius had fallen already. Most of the runners were in far better shape and even the fittest of the slaves now appeared to be slowing. It seemed that several had had the same idea as Decimus, and were pacing themselves well. However, one or two others were doing just the opposite.

Up ahead, Decimus finally spotted Ruma and Olu, who seemed to be taking turns to outrun each other. It was a good idea, and Decimus didn't doubt the wily Etrurian had thought of it. A little way back from the sprinting duo, Argon was hobbling slightly from a badly burned heel.

The next slave to fall was a tall boy with

dark skin and fair hair. He gave no yell or outward cry of despair, but he collapsed nevertheless, and curled into a ball as the servants hoisted him into their arms.

Decimus returned his attention to Teo, who was now spearheading the race and moving away from his nearest rival. Unfortunately, Teo made the mistake of glancing back over his shoulder, and the coals claimed him. He let out a terrible cry, grabbed for his burning foot and collapsed. He was hauled away, but not before the next five slaves had all leapt over him. When the last of these stumbled, going face first into a nasty collection of smouldering embers, Mori held up a hand and signalled that the trial had ended.

Fifty boys were led back to the cells.

Miraculously, Gladius was one of them.

CHAPTER
IV

COMBAT

The mood in the cells that night was bleak. Argon just slumped on his bed, staring at the wall: he pretty much ignored his soup when the bowls were brought round. Decimus made it clear that he couldn't understand quite why the Gaul was so upset about the elimination of his cellmate, but Gladius suspected that the two had been brought in together, just like himself and Decimus.

'They'd probably formed a friendship,' he whispered to his stern companion. 'I mean, look at us – we're friends now, right?'

Decimus shrugged.

'Oh come on,' Gladius persisted. 'If we weren't friends, you'd never have given me that advice before the race . . . and the chances are I wouldn't have made it, either.'

The fact was, not only had Gladius made it through the first round of the trials, he was also largely unharmed. It came as no small surprise to Decimus that there seemed to be remarkably few burns on Gladius's feet: it was almost as if he'd managed to dodge every coal. Decimus couldn't help but grin as he saw his friend throw a victory punch at the air – Gladius might be unfit and very frightened, but he certainly knew when to take good advice.

Decimus looked down at his own feet, which were scorched in so many places that it even hurt when he twitched his toes. Evidently, you needed more than good tactics to escape a trial unharmed – luck also played a significant part.

In the far cell, Ruma and Olu were locked in conversation. At first, Decimus was suspicious that they might be plotting some sort of escape, or creating a combined strategy for the trials ahead. However, he soon dismissed these thoughts – there was no chance of escape from Arena Primus, and the trials were totally unpredictable. The two slaves were probably just talking about Teo's fate in the underground prisons, and didn't want Argon to overhear them.

A dark and depressing night ensued.

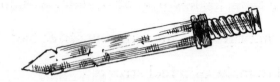

The following morning, Decimus woke early

and managed to drag himself out of bed in order to get in some exercise. He was particularly pleased when he saw that Ruma and Olu were both still fast asleep, and this spurred him to try even harder to stretch himself.

By the time Jailer Truli arrived with their breakfast, he had already completed more than a hundred sit-ups and had even tried the bizarre headstand exercise he'd seen Olu doing the morning before. He tried to run on the spot for a time, but the agonizing pain in his feet had become a dull ache that was proving to be even worse. Still, there was no doubt that the early morning exercises had helped to make him feel strong.

When breakfast was over and Truli

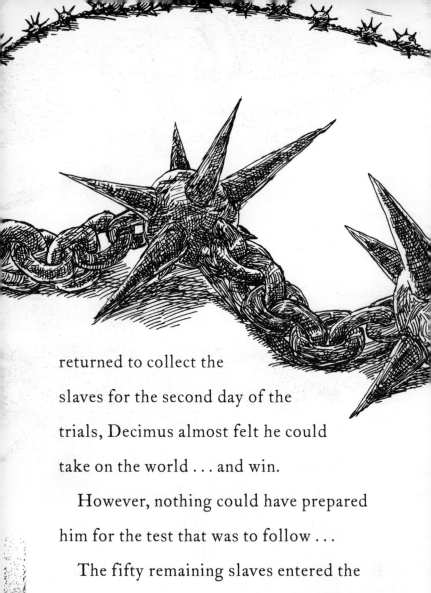

returned to collect the

slaves for the second day of the

trials, Decimus almost felt he could

take on the world . . . and win.

However, nothing could have prepared

him for the test that was to follow . . .

The fifty remaining slaves entered the

arena to a very different scene. Decimus

noticed that a large circle had been marked

out in the middle of the arena floor,
but he couldn't quite tell what it was made
of. When he said as much to Gladius, the big
slave edged a little closer to try to make out
more details.

'Spikes, I'm guessing,' Ruma said,

appearing beside Gladius with a concerned look on his face. 'A chain full of spikes, laid down in a ring. These trial-masters really have it in for our feet, don't they?'

'It seems so,' Decimus agreed, eyeing the Etrurian with respect. 'What do you think the contest will be?'

Ruma shrugged. 'Some sort of combat, I'm guessing. Looks like we're about to find out . . .'

The three trial-masters emerged from the eastern portcullis, but this time it was Mori and Falni who took to the stalls.

Hrin, the tall and impossibly thin master,

stepped forward and raised his bony hands.
He was holding a large black sack.

'Today's trial will only require two
combatants,' he screeched. 'The rest of you
will observe. Now . . . form a line. When I
come to you, you will reach into the bag and
pick out a single ball. If you receive a white
ball, you will step forward: if the ball you
pick is black, you may take a step back.'

When the slaves had organized
themselves, Hrin strode up to the boy at the
distant end of the line, and held out the sack.
Decimus tried to lean forward in order to see
the ball being drawn, but it seemed that every

slave in the line had had the same idea . . .
and he couldn't tell what was happening
until the boy – a muscular youth with a
distinctive Roman nose – stepped back.

'Lucky start,' Gladius whispered.

'Not really,' said Ruma, on Decimus's
other side. 'If they only need a couple of
combatants, it means that there are forty-
eight black balls and just two white ones.
You'd have to be really unlucky to pull those
out.'

'Bet I get one,' Gladius whinged.

Decimus was quite surprised when his
friend's comment caused Olu and Argon to
burst out
laughing, but
the merriment

quickly died away when Hrin barked
something from the end of the line.

Decimus leaned forward again: the
skeletal trial-master was now more than
twenty boys along, and there was still no sign
of a white ball. As Hrin moved on, more and
more boys stepped back, and there were
several audible sighs of relief.

Then, finally, a white ball was drawn.

The unfortunate selector, a heavy-set boy
with greasy black hair and several bruises
around his jaw, didn't even flinch. He simply
looked down at the small sphere in his hand,
and gritted his teeth.

'He's called Boma Derok,' Gladius whispered. 'He was standing next to me in the coal race.'

Decimus took a deep breath as the slave stepped forward and Hrin moved on. The gangly trial-master was now only four places away.

Olu drew a black ball, and stepped back. He was followed by Argon and Ruma. When it came to Gladius's turn, Decimus actually found himself holding his breath . . . but his friend pulled out a black sphere, and withdrew from the line.

Again, Hrin moved on.

Decimus plunged his arm into the sack, and felt his mind go numb.

1 . . . 2 . . . 3 . . . now.

He withdrew his hand, and heard the gasps

from his side before he'd
even had time to look
down.

He was holding a
white ball: the draw was
complete.

'You can all step back,'
said Hrin, pointing to the
line of six or seven boys who'd
been standing to the left of
Decimus. They quickly obeyed
the trial-master, and the heart of
the arena suddenly became an
incredibly lonely place.

Decimus glanced to his right . . .
and stared into the determined
face of his opponent.

'You two will fight in there,' Hrin commanded, pointing toward the ring of spikes. 'The first of you to fall outside the circle will be eliminated from the trials.' He turned back to the snaking line of slaves. 'The rest of you, watch and be thankful you have escaped this test.'

The two slaves entered the ring of spikes and began to circle each other warily.

Decimus clenched his fists. His heart was thumping in his chest and his breath caught in his throat: he'd never been in a fight before, if you excluded one or two minor scuffles with his cousins, and now he was about to enter into deadly combat. His hands were shaking, but he couldn't tell if it was fear or excitement forcing the reaction.

He was still deciding whether to run at Boma Derok when the muscular slave made the decision for him, and roared across the sand like a rogue lion. He cannoned into

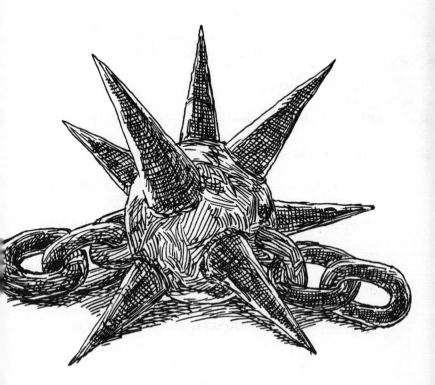

Decimus and lifted him off the ground, blocking the smaller slave's attempts to drive a knee into his ribcage.

Glancing back over his shoulder, Decimus saw that the edge of the circle was nearing. He bunched his hands into fists and brought them both down with all his might on his opponent's back.

Boma staggered slightly, and Decimus felt the grip around his midsection relax. Seizing the initiative, he brought up his knee in a second attempt to strike Boma's ribcage. This time, he was successful: the big slave dropped him ... mere inches from the edge of the circle.

Boma didn't waste any time. Still reeling from the blow to his ribs, he quickly took

several steps back and crouched a ready

stance. Decimus charged at him

and the two slaves

clashed in the middle of the ring.

Boma threw out two punches that both went wild as the quicker, smaller slave ducked and dodged past him. In turn, Decimus tried to grapple Boma in a headlock but was shoved back with such force that he actually stumbled.

The fight was accompanied by rounds of cheers and sighs from the slave line, most of whom seemed to be rooting for Boma. Decimus could just make out the distant shape of Gladius waving his arms and jumping up and down on the spot.

Decimus returned his attention to Boma, just in time to see the big slave go for a

second mad charge. Instinctively, he dropped to the ground, sweeping his legs around just as Boma tried and failed to stop his own momentum. Decimus wriggled out of the way as his opponent came crashing on to the sand, but was completely taken by surprise when Boma immediately shot out an arm and slammed it across his chest.

While Decimus rolled over and clutched at his bruised front, the big slave leapt to his feet and loomed over him.

Decimus winced as a powerful hand clamped around his throat and lifted him bodily off the ground. Kicking and punching with all his might, he nevertheless felt

completely powerless as Boma held him aloft, slowly stalking towards the edge of the ring with a renewed determination.

Was this the end for Decimus Rex . . . ?

COMING SOON

More terrifying trials await Decimus Rex in the dreaded Arena of Doom, from jumping between small wooden platforms on sky-high poles to being attacked by giants with hammers. As each trial eliminates more and more boys, Decimus becomes desperate to escape. Can he survive against the best of his fellow slaves? More importantly, will he be forced to meet one of his new friends in combat? Find out in . . .

ESCAPE FROM EVIL

COMING SOON

DAVID GRIMSTONE

GLADIATOR BOY

A HERO'S QUEST

DAVID GRIMSTONE

GLADIATOR BOY

ESCAPE FROM EVIL

FREE GLADIATOR GAME INSIDE

DAVID GRIMSTONE

GLADIATOR BOY

STOWAWAY SLAVES

FREE GLADIATOR GAME INSIDE

DAVID GRIMSTONE

GLADIATOR BOY

THE REBELS' ASSAULT

FREE GLADIATOR GAME INSIDE

DAVID GRIMSTONE

GLADIATOR BOY

THE BLADE OF FIRE

FREE GLADIATOR GAME INSIDE

DAVID GRIMSTONE

GLADIATOR BOY

RESCUE MISSION

FREE GLADIATOR GAME INSIDE

ARENA COMBAT

Get ready to challenge your friends! Each Gladiator Boy book will contain a different trial – collect them all to run your own Arena of Doom – either at home or in the school playground.

TRIAL 1
SWORD, GAUNTLET, HAMMER!

You will need two players and one referee. This game is like the traditional scissors – paper – stone game. Each attack must be presented at exactly the same time and then worked out. The first player to win 3 games out of 5 is declared the winner!

You can either play the game as yourselves or, when you have collected all the Decimus Rex books, you can take on the roles of the gladiatorial slaves and use their special character profiles to fire your imagination! One such profile can be found on the next two pages and there will be more in the other Gladiator Boy books!

Here are the hand signs:

1. THE SWORD

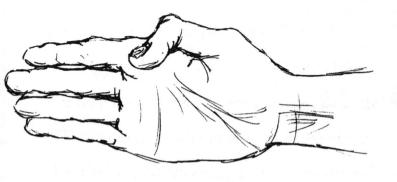

2. THE GAUNTLET

3. THE HAMMER

RESULTS GRID		
WEAPON	BEATS	IS DEFEATED BY
Hammer	Sword	Gauntlet
Sword	Gauntlet	Hammer
Gauntlet	Hammer	Sword

CHARACTER PROFILE
OLU

NAME: Olu

FROM: Africa

HEIGHT: 1.77 metres

BODY TYPE: Slim

BEST FRIEND: Argon

CELLMATE: Ruma

OLU QUIZ: How well do you know Olu? Can you answer the following three questions?

1. WHO MAKES OLU BURST OUT LAUGHING?

2. WHAT IS OLU'S FAVOURITE EXERCISE, WHICH DECIMUS ALSO TRIES?

3. WHO DOES OLU TAKES TURNS TO OUT-RUN IN THE COAL RACE?

WEAPON
PROFILE
THE SWORD

A sword is a long, shaped piece of metal. It was used as a weapon in many historical battles and has appeared in more battle stories than any other weapon, ever!

There are many types of sword and each one can be used in different ways. Here are the most common ways to fight with a sword.

SINGLE HAND

DOUBLE HAND

TWO SWORDS

SPECIAL ATTACK – THE WHIRLING DOOM

READ MORE OF DECIMUS REX'S ADVENTURES IN BOOK TWO OF THE GLADIATOR BOY SERIES:

ESCAPE FROM EVIL

Decimus closed his eyes. Surrounded by a ring of spikes, he was fighting for his life against a fellow slave. He wasn't sure he was going to make it. Locked in a powerful choke hold and lifted from the ground, Decimus found himself rushed towards the edge of the combat circle in the mammoth hands of Boma Derok.

Screaming with rage, Decimus shifted his weight several times to no avail – the big slave was so strong that it was like trying to struggle against a moving boulder.

The two combatants had nearly reached the spikes when Decimus suddenly snaked down a hand and raked his fingernails across Boma's eyes. The big slave dropped his opponent immediately, and raised both hands to his scratched face.

Decimus landed on his feet, hopped around behind the wounded fighter and threw all his weight at him. Boma staggered forward, palms still covering his eyes, and tripped on the line of spikes. He was doomed.

As the fickle slave crowd roared its approval, Boma Derok plunged face-first into the sand.

The combat was over.

Decimus wasn't quite prepared for the admiration and cheers he received that night in the cell section. Gladius couldn't stop talking about the fight, Olu and Ruma both offered Decimus their own soup and even Argon reached through the bars and shook his hand. Further down the corridor, whispers and distant shouts could be heard: the name Decimus was spreading along the corridors like wildfire. Boma Derok's fate would now be a subject few discussed, his name forgotten by all but his cellmate and presumably – in some distant town – by his family. Meanwhile, he would rot in the underground prisons.

Decimus knew he could easily have suffered the same destiny and, to Gladius's surprise, decided to scratch the big slave's name into the cell floor with his spoon. Boma didn't deserve to be forgotten: no one did.

'There's something going on out there.'

At first, Decimus thought the words had been spoken by Gladius, but his friend was staring past him. Turning, he saw that his eyes were on Ruma, who had squeezed himself against the barred door of his cell and was straining to see down the far end of the corridor. Behind him, Olu had drifted off to sleep.

'What's up?' said Argon, getting to his feet and heading across to the front of his own cell.

'Whispers,' said Ruma, holding up a hand in order to keep the others quiet. 'Apparently, there's a lot of noise coming from the arena.'

'Fighting?' Decimus asked, sharing a hopeful glance with Gladius.

Ruma shook his head. 'No, more like building; you know, hammering and work noise.'

Argon was now pressed against the barred door separating his cell from the corridor. 'What's that?' he said.

'Just wait,' snapped Ruma, as Olu began to stir. 'I can't hear anything with you talk—'

'No, not the noise – what is that?'

Ruma tried to follow Argon's pointing finger and squinted into the shadows. 'I don't know what you're looking at!'

'On the wall! Just up the corridor!' Argon sneaked a hand through the bars and extended his finger as far as it would reach. 'THERE!'

Ruma squinted harder. 'Keys,' he said, eventually. 'It's a hook – Truli keeps his ring of cell keys on it.'

'Can you get to it?' Gladius hazarded.

Ruma laughed. 'Are you crazy? Do you think I have ropes for arms or something?'

They all burst into fits of laughter ... but Decimus said nothing. He was staring very thoughtfully into the shadows.

When the slave horde arrived in the arena the following morning, Master Falni had taken control of the trials. From what Decimus could tell, this wasn't good news: a series of giant poles had been erected, each supporting a circular wooden platform at its summit.

'They get smaller and smaller,' said Ruma, his sharp eyes taking in the scene before him. 'And they also get further apart.'

Decimus nodded. He had spotted a ladder

next to the distant pole supporting the largest platform. It didn't take a genius to work out what was expected of the slaves.

'I notice Slavious Doom never watches any of the trials,' Olu whispered. He spoke so rarely that his voice caused everyone to turn towards him. 'At least, if he is watching I haven't seen him.'

'No,' Decimus agreed. 'He hasn't been here. I'm thinking he probably won't show up until the end of the trials.'

'Ha!' Argon exclaimed. 'Then the chances are none of us will ever see him.'

'Decimus might,' said Gladius, without a trace of humour in his voice.

'Yeah,' admitted Ruma, smiling. 'Decimus might.'

GLADIATOR BOY

Check out the Gladiator Boy website for games, downloads, activities, sneak previews and lots of fun! You can even get extra pieces of the arena and fantastic action figures! Sign up to the newsletter to receive exclusive extra content and the opportunity to enter special competitions.

WWW.GLADIATORBOY.COM

LET BATTLE COMMENCE!

MAKE YOUR OWN ARENA OF DOOM

1. Carefully cut around the outline of the arena section. Ask an adult to help if necessary.
2. Fold across line A. Use a ruler to get a straight edge.
3. Fold across line B. Use a ruler to get a straight edge.
4. Ask an adult to help you score along lines C & D with a pair of sharp scissors.
5. Fold up over line E and push the window out.
6. Repeat instructions 1 to 5 for every Arena of Doom piece collected.
7. Glue the top of each tab and stick them to the next piece of the arena. Repeat as necessary.

CHECK OUT THE WEBSITE FOR A PHOTO OF THE COMPLETE ARENA.

TO MAKE YOUR ACTION FIGURE

1. Cut around the outline of the figure. Ask an adult to help if necessary.
2. Cut along slot X at the bottom of the figure.
3. Cut out Gladiator Boy rectangle.
4. Cut along slot Y.
5. Slot figure into slot Y.

cut along the lines

cut along the lines Y

GLADIATOR BOY
WWW.GLADIATORBOY.COM

Cut out the character and arena section along the black lines. Using the instructions opposite make your own Arena of Doom.

Hodder Children's Books

GLADIATOR BOY

WWW.GLADIATORBOY.COM

Hodder Children's Books